SAM'S SNEAKER SEARCH

BY CLAIRE O'BRIEN • ILLUSTRATED BY CHARLES FUGE

Simon & Schuster Books for Young Readers

SIMON & SCHUSTER BOOKS FOR YOUNG READERS

An imprint of Simon & Schuster Children's Publishing Division

1230 Avenue of the Americas

New York, New York 10020

SIMON & SCHUSTER BOOKS FOR YOUNG READERS is a trademark of Simon & Schuster.

Book design by Heather Wood

The text of this book is set in Century

The illustrations are rendered in watercolor

Printed and bound in Singapore

First Edition

1 3 5 7 9 10 8 6 4 2

Library of Congress Cataloging-in-Publication Data

O'Brien, Claire.

Sam's sneaker search / by Claire O'Brien ; illustrated by Charles Fuge.—1st ed.

p.   cm.

Summary : After searching throughout the house for her one lost sneaker,

Samantha decides that she can't wear it after all.

ISBN 0-689-80169-6 (hc)

[1. Sneakers—Fiction. 2. Lost and found possessions—Fiction.

3. Shoes—Fiction.] I. Fuge, Charles, ill. II. Title.

PZ7.O12675Sam   1997   [E]—dc20   96-2964   CIP   AC

For Mr. and Mrs. Ikeda C O

To Vicki C F

"Where's your other sneaker?" Samantha's mother shouted up the stairs. "It's a quarter to nine and you're going to be late for school."

The first place Sam looked was in her
bedroom. No sneaker under the bed, just
a shaggy lion playing with the dust mice.

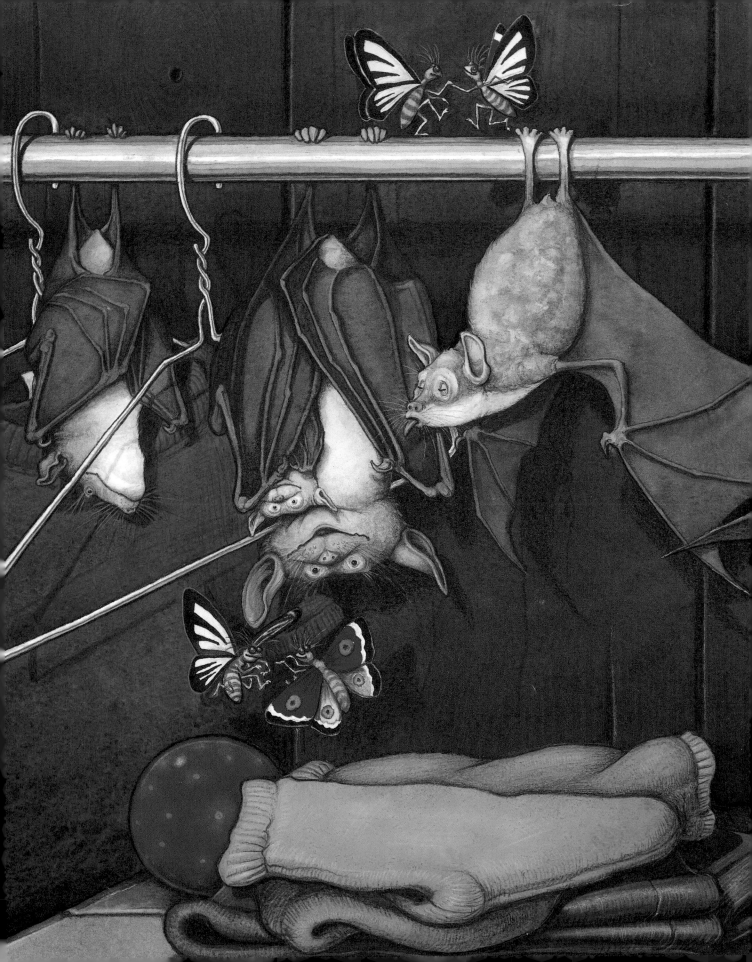

No sneaker at the back of the closet, just
a family of bats watching the moths dance.

No sneaker in the toy box, just a
woolly sheep lazily grazing.

So Samantha looked in the bathroom (as soon as it was free). No sneaker behind the sink, just a huge python squeezing the toothpaste.

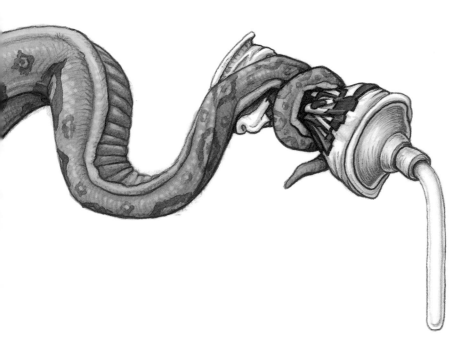

No sneaker down the toilet, just
a giant octopus sailing toy boats.

No sneaker in the bathtub, just a hippopotamus blowing bubbles.

Next Sam looked in the kitchen. No sneaker on the shelf, just a hen minding her chicks.

No sneaker inside the fridge, just a pair of penguins skating on the Jell-O.

No sneaker under the table,

just a hungry bear searching for scraps.

So Samantha looked in the living room.
No sneaker beside the television, just a
kangaroo watching the news.

"Excuse me," said the kangaroo, "but have you lost something?"

"Yes, my sneaker. It's red, like this one. See?" Sam showed her sneaker to the kangaroo.

"I'm sure I saw one like that on the doorstep."

"Oh, good. Thanks," said Sam, and she dashed to see.

There, outside the front door, was her sneaker, all chewed up and torn.

"Oh, drat," said Samantha. "That billy goat's been here again."

So she had to look for her sandals.